The
Gigantic
Turnip

For Owen — N. S.

Barefoot Beginners
an imprint of
Barefoot Books
PO Box 95
Kingswood
Bristol BS30 5BH

Illustrations copyright © 1998 by Niamh Sharkey

The moral right of Niamh Sharkey to be identified as the illustrator
of this work has been asserted.

Hardcover ISBN 1 902283 11 2
Paperback ISBN 1 902283 29 5

Graphic design by Tom Grzelinski, Bath
Colour reproduction by Grafiscan, Verona
Printed in Singapore by Tien Wah Press (Pte) Ltd

3 5 7 9 8 6 4

The Gigantic Turnip

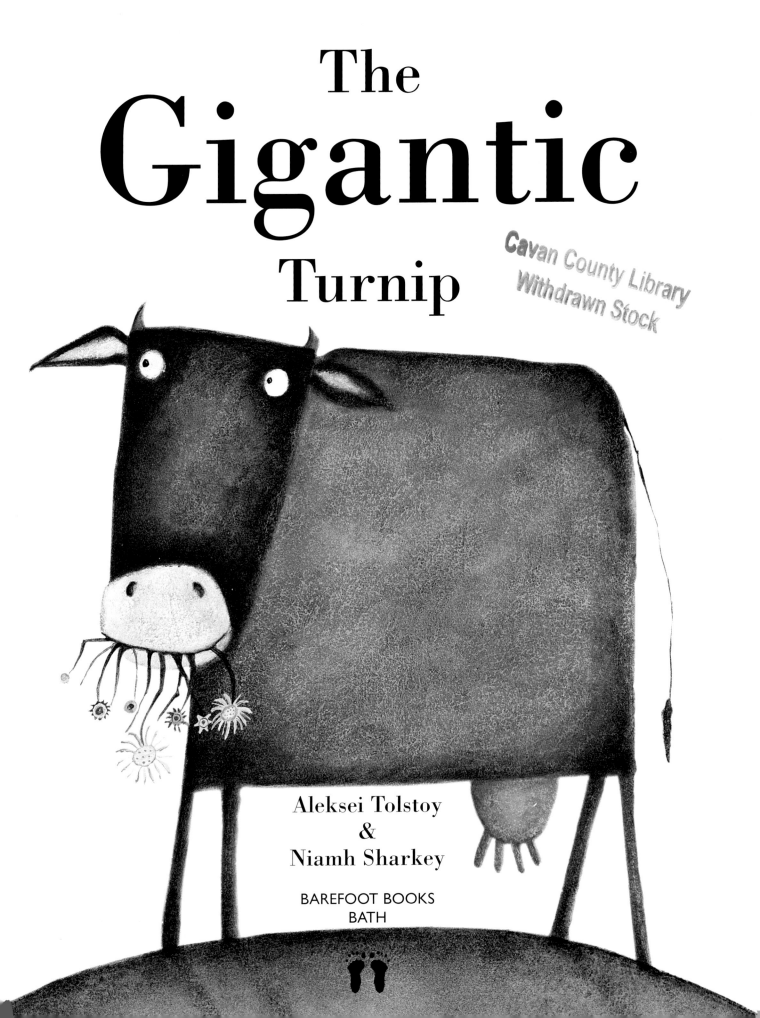

Aleksei Tolstoy
&
Niamh Sharkey

BAREFOOT BOOKS
BATH

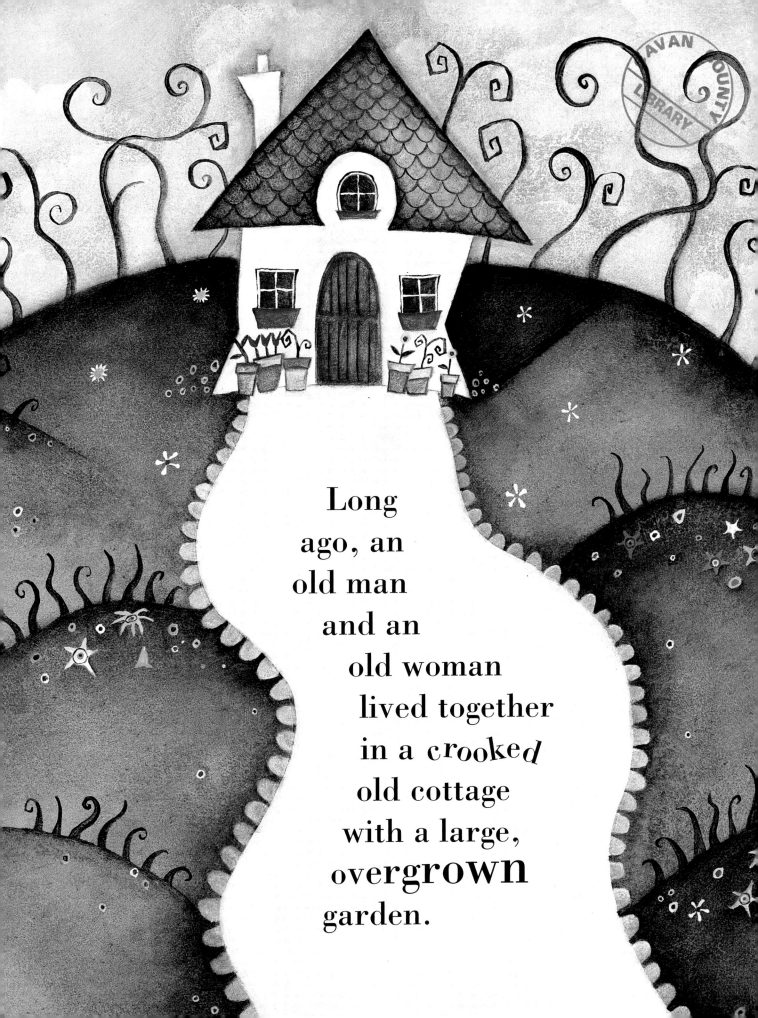

Long ago, an old man and an old woman lived together in a crooked old cottage with a large, overgrown garden.

The old man
and the old
woman

kept six yellow canaries,

five white geese,

four speckled hens,

three black cats,

two pot-bellied pigs

and one big brown cow.

On a fine March morning, the
old woman sat up in bed, sniffed
the sweet spring air and said,
'It's time for us to sow the
vegetables!' So the old man
and the old woman went out
into the garden.

They sowed peas and carrots and potatoes and beans. Last of all, they sowed turnips.

That night, rain fell — pitter, patter! —
on the garden of the crooked old cottage.
The old man and the old woman smiled as
they slept.

The rain would help the seeds swell and produce fine juicy vegetables.

Spring passed and the summer sun ripened the vegetables. The old man and the old woman harvested their carrots and potatoes and peas and beans and turnips. At the end of the row, there was just one turnip left. It looked very big.
In fact, it looked

gigantic.

On a fine
September
morning, the
old man sat up
in bed, sniffed
the cool autumn
air and said,
'It's time for us to
pull up that turnip.'

And out he went.

The old man pulled and
heaved and tugged and
yanked, but the turnip
would not move.

The old man went to find
the old woman.

The old woman wrapped her arms round the old man's waist. Both of them pulled and heaved and tugged and yanked, but still the turnip would not move.

So the old woman went to fetch the big brown cow.

The old man, the old woman and the big brown cow pulled and heaved and tugged and yanked, but still the turnip would not move.

So the old man mopped his brow and went to fetch the two pot-bellied pigs.

The old man, the old woman, the big brown cow and the two pot-bellied pigs pulled and heaved and tugged and yanked. Still the turnip would not move.

So the old woman rolled up her sleeves and went to fetch the three black cats.

The old man, the old woman, the big brown cow, the two pot-bellied pigs and the three black cats pulled and heaved and tugged and yanked. Still the turnip would not move.

So one of the cats twitched her tail and went to fetch the four speckled hens.

The old man, the old
woman, the big brown
cow, the two pot-bellied
pigs, the three black cats
and the four speckled
hens pulled and heaved
and tugged and yanked.
Still the turnip would
not move.

So one of the hens shook
her feathers and went to
fetch the five white geese.

The old man, the old woman, the big brown cow, the two pot-bellied pigs, the three black cats, the four speckled hens and the five white geese pulled and heaved and tugged and yanked. Still the turnip would not move.

So one of the geese
craned her neck and
went to fetch the
six yellow canaries.

The old man, the old woman, the big brown cow, the two pot-bellied pigs, the three black cats, the four speckled hens,

the five white geese and the
six yellow canaries pulled
and heaved and tugged
and yanked.

Still the turnip would not move.

The old man scratched his head.

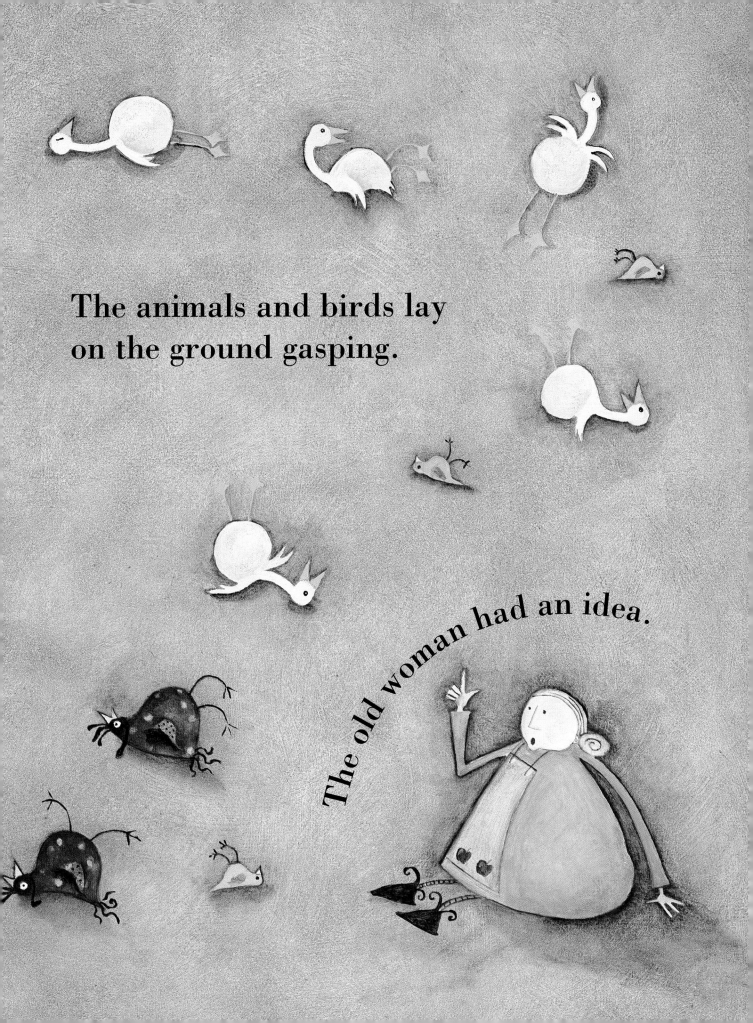

The animals and birds lay on the ground gasping.

The old woman had an idea.

The old woman went into the kitchen and put a piece of cheese by the mousehole. Soon a hungry little mouse popped its head out of the hole. The old woman caught the mouse and carried it outside.

The old man, the old woman, the big brown cow, the two pot-bellied pigs, the three black cats, the four speckled hens,

the five white geese, the
six yellow canaries and the
hungry little mouse pulled
and heaved and tugged
and yanked.

Pop!

The gigantic turnip came flying out of the ground and everyone fell over. The canaries fell on the mouse, the geese fell on the canaries, the hens fell on the geese, the cats fell on the hens, the pigs fell on the cats, the cow fell on the pigs, the old woman fell on the cow and the old man fell on the old woman.

All of them lay on the ground and laughed.

That night the old man and
the old woman made a huge
bowl of turnip stew.
Everyone ate as much as
they could. And do you know
what? The hungry little
mouse ate the most of all.

BAREFOOT BOOKS publishes high-quality picture books for
children of all ages and specialises in the work of artists and writers from
many cultures. If you have enjoyed this book and would like to receive a copy of
our current catalogue, please contact our London office — tel: 0171 704 6492
fax: 0171 359 5798 email: sales@barefoot-books.com
website: www.barefoot-books.com